Queen Calafia!

THE REAL QUEEN OF CALIFORNIA. A SLAYER OF INJUSTICE. A WARRIOR OF LOVE. HER MAJESTY THE QUEEN CALAFIA HAS BEEN RESUSCITATED FROM THE PROVINCE OF AL-ANDALUSIAN SPAIN. DETHRONED IN AMERICA, AND THEN RESURRECTED FROM THE EVILS OF WHITEWASH AND SUPPRESSION OF HISTORY. HER MAJESTY, "CALAFIA", IS THE TRUE "QUEEN OF CALIFORNIA". THE PARADISE ISLAND WHICH HOUSED THE MOST BEAUTIFUL, COURAGEOUS, POWERFUL AND ENTERPRISING BLACK WOMEN IN HISTORY. A TRUE WONDER HER MAJESTY IS! FOR THE FIRST TIME IN AMERICAN HISTORY, HER MAJESTY THE QUEEN HAS RISEN TO FIGHT, AS HER ANCESTORS BEFORE HER, AGAINST EVIL. FLANKED BY GRIFFINS AND ARMED WITH GOLD WEAPONS TO RECLAIM HER RIGHTFUL THRONE. RISING TO BREAK THE GLASS WALLS OF CONFINEMENT THAT SUSTAINED CENTURIES OF OPPRESSION AGAINST HER PEOPLE!

CREATED BY TAMRA L. CALIFORNIA DICUS
BASED ON THE NOVEL BY GARCÍ RODRÍGUEZ DE MONTALVO
DISCLAIMER: EVERYTHING HEREIN IS NOT OF THE FEDERAL GOVERNMENT NOR THE USPTO.

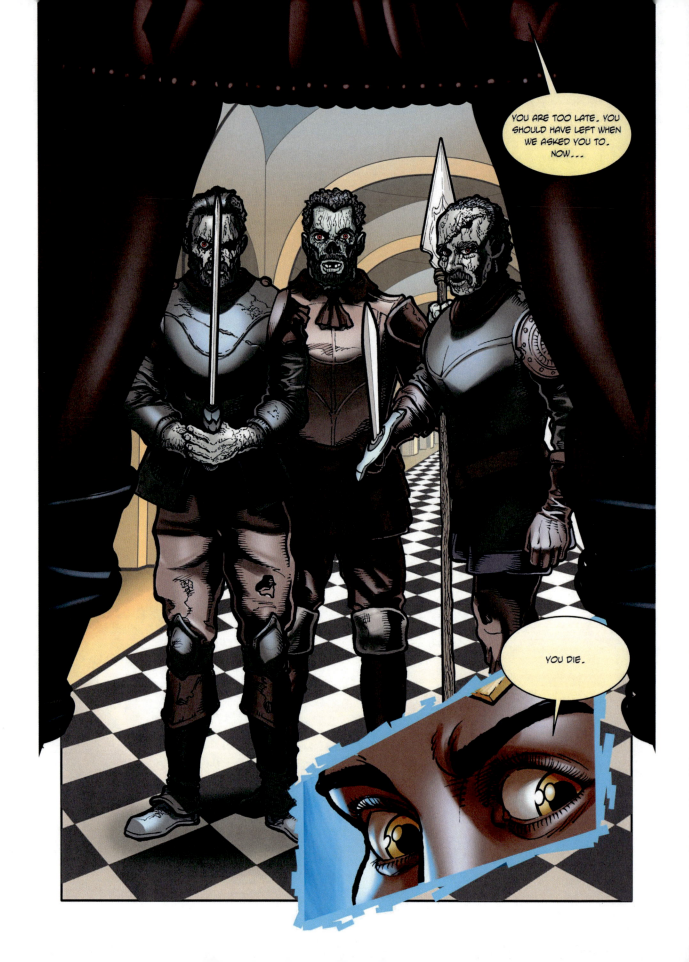

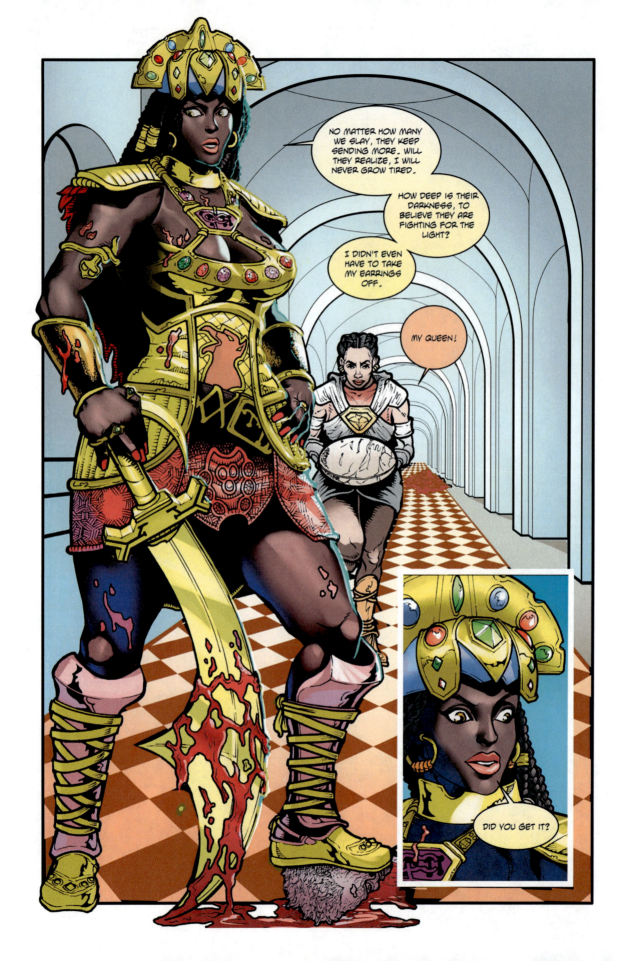

CALIFORNIA IS ME® PRESENTS

Queen Calafia™
Queen of California™

CREATOR Co-WRITER:	MS. TAMRA L. CALIFORNIA DICUS	WASHINGTON, D.C.
BASED ON THE NOVEL BY:	GARCÍ RODRÍGUEZ DE MONTALVO	SPAIN
Co-WRITER:	MR. COREY MARSHALL	NEW YORK
ILLUSTRATOR:	MR. ROBERT ROACH	CALIFORNIA
DIGITAL ARTIST-COLORIST:	MR. TOYIN AJETUNMOBI	NIGERIA
LOGO DESIGNER:	MR. ITHAN PAYNE	FLORIDA

ΣCA = MUJERES NEGRAS + BELLA + VALIENTE + PODEROSA + EMPRENDEDORA
ΣCA = BLACK WOMEN + BEAUTIFUL + COURAGEOUS + POWERFUL + ENTERPRISING

OH, MY DEAR READER, THE TIME HAS COME TO WIELD THE PEN TO HONOR THE HIDDEN QUEENS – THE BLACK WOMAN AND HER OFFSPRING NOT ONLY IN AMERICA, BUT WORLDWIDE. I WISH I COULD SAY I AM 100% EXCITED TO PRESENT THIS BODY OF WORK. HOWEVER, I HAVE MIXED FEELINGS. FROM FEAR, TO WORRY, TO LOVE TO HATE. I HAVE TAKEN EVERY EFFORT TO GRAB THE BEST WITHIN MY LIMITED RESOURCES TO PRODUCE FOR AMERICAN HISTORY, THE FIRST EVER QUEEN CALAFIA QUEEN OF CALIFORNIA COMIC BOOK TO CONTINUE IN THE LIGHT OF ITS REGAL, CHOCOLATE, AL-ANDALUSIAN SPANISH ORIGIN.

WHAT HAPPENED?   WHAT'S GOING ON?

THE FIGHT IS REAL, FOR THE DESCENDANTS OF NEAR GENOCIDE AND ENSLAVEMENT. WE UNDERSTAND FROM HISTORY THAT BLACK INTELLIGENCE CAN BE PERCEIVED AS DANGEROUS. IT IS NOT A JOKE. IT IS NOT COMICAL. THIS MEDIUM WAS DEEMED BEST TO REVIVE THE STORY OF CALAFIA'S CALIFORNIA. I PRAY IT IS FUN, BUT ALSO AWAKENS CHANGE FOR A BETTER FUTURE FOR AFRICAN DESCENDANTS AND ALL OF US. MAY IT BE A TOOL TO HELP ILLUMINATE THE MIND, RESONATE THE SOUL, AND PASS IN SPIRIT FOR OUR RESTORATIVE LEGACY. HISTORY UNFOLDS THE LINEAGE OF PLETHORA OF AFRICAN TRIBES BEFORE; WE, BLACK WOMEN, PUT THE "W" IN "WARRIORS"! QUEEN CALAFIA IS THE LEGENDARY PRECURSOR TO POPULARIZED AMERICAN COMICS. SO, WE DEMAND OUR CREDIT. THIS BODY OF WORK WAS ONLY MADE POSSIBLE BY THE COURAGE AND SKILL OF QUEENS AND KINGS, INCLUSIVE OF MY FAMILY AND FRIENDS, INQUISITIVE CHILDREN TO LAWYERS TO ENGINEERS TO HISTORIANS AND LIBRARIANS THAT MOTIVATED ME TO CONTINUE TO FIGHT INJUSTICE. WE MUST THINK CRITICALLY 2 SURVIVE. THIS AMERICAN GEM FROM THE BLACK MALE REIGN THAT SPANS AFRICA TO EUROPE, IS NOW UNVEILED IN COLOR SINCE THE AGE OF EXPLORATION AND THE AMERICAN ERAS OF WARS, TO NO LONGER SHUN BUT UPLIFT THE STRENGTH OF THE BLACK WOMAN – THE AMERICAN BEDROCK, THE ROOT OF THE NAME "CALIFORNIA" AND HER MAJESTY CALAFIA – REMINISCENT OF THE DEBT LONG OVERDUE BY THE UNJUSTLY ENRICHED BENEFACTORS. HONOR THE PAST & CARE 4 THE FUTURE OF THE BLACK INDIGENOUS PEOPLE OF COLOR! CA=STRONGEST IN THE WORLD!!

WHY DID NOT POWERS CARVE HER MAJESTY CALAFIA OUT OF BLACK EGYPTIAN MARBLES?

FOOD FOR THOUGHT
WHAT TALE FOR TALE COPY VERSION IS OUT NOW?
BREAK BARRIERS & RESTORE THE PEOPLE & JUSTICE

DO YOU SEE THE CALIFORNIA WARRIORS AS DEFINED ANYWHERE?

#RISE: RECTIFY INAUGURATE STABILIZE EQUALIZE (THANKS QK!)
#CALIISME #JUSTICE4QUEENCALAFIA+CA #BLACKQUEENMAGIC

εύρηκαμεν!!
4EEH

¡VIVA REINA CALAFIA! LONG LIVE THE QUEEN CALAFIA!
RISE, SLAY AND RULE MY CALIFORNIA WARRIORS!
-Ms. Tamra, Founder of California Is Me ®

STOP THE PROPAGANDA OF HISTORY!

THIS PUBLICATION IS ™, ®, AND ©- ALL RIGHTS RESERVED.
QUEEN CALAFIA ™ QUEEN OF CALIFORNIA™
CALIFORNIA IS ME ® © 2022. MADE IN THE USA.
100% BLACK AND FEMALE OWNED AND OPERATED.

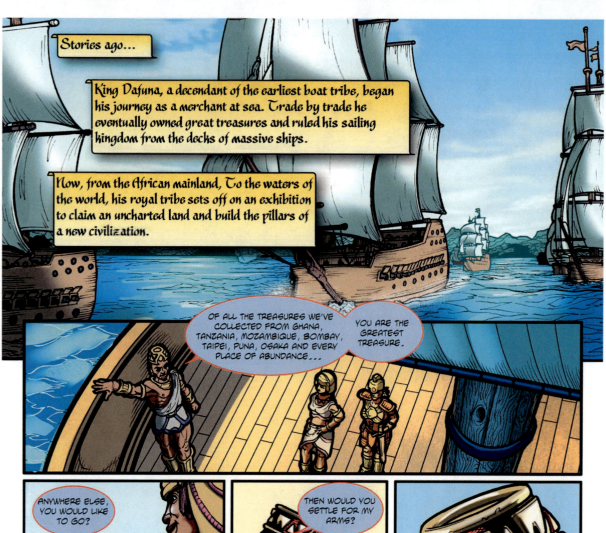

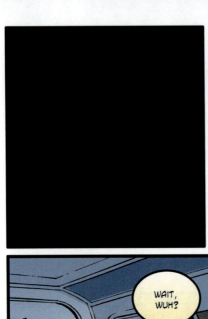

LONG, LONG AGO IN A DISTANT TIME, THE ANCIENT STORIES INFORM US OF THE TRUE HISTORY OF OUR AFRICAN ANCESTORS. THEY WERE THE FIRST NAVIGATORS OF ROYAL QUEENS AND KINGS TO SAIL TO THE AMERICAS PRIOR TO COLUMBUS. PRIOR TO MIXING WITH THE COLORED INDIGENOUS, SOME BECAME ENSLAVED, AND OTHERS WERE SELF-EMANCIPATED. THIS COVERT, GOLDEN BRIDGE OF INFORMATION, ONCE OPAQUE AS STORMY CLOUDS, HAS RISEN TO THE SURFACE REMINDING US OF OUR GOLDEN AFRICAN GEMS AND ROYAL REIGN. WE NEED OUR SYMBOLS OF FREEDOM NOT ENSLAVEMENT. TOGETHER, WE THE PEOPLE, SHALL WIELD THE POWER OF SOCIAL MEDIA TO PETITION FOR THE ARGUABLY MISREPRESENTED STATE INSIGNIA TO BE CORRECTED DUE TO ENSLAVEMENT. THIS IS A CREATIVE CRY FOR A CALL TO ACTION WHERE WE MAY ALL PARTICIPATE IN MAKING HISTORY!

CALAFIA

STAY TUNED FOR THE NEXT QUEEN CALAFIA COMING SOON.
SEE WWW.CALIFORNIAISME.COM OR WWW.CALIISME.COM
WWW.CALIFORNIAGREATSEAL.COM FOR MORE INFORMATION. FOLLOW US ON SOCIAL MEDIA, SIGN PETITIONS, GRAB GEAR AND COMMENT USING HASHTAGS: #RISE #CALIISME #JUSTICE4QC+CA #BLACKQUEENMAGIC

LIFTING THE VEIL OF IGNORANCE: SPECIAL THANKS 2 LAW AND HISTORY PROFESSORS: ALKEBULAN, BISHOM-RAPP, BULLOCK, DYSON, GREENE, SEMERARO, + WILDENTHAL + STUDENTS AT TJSL, SAN DIEGO, CA + ALL IN AL, CA, TX, D.C. DMV, KS, MO, GA, FL, PA, + NY. THE CIM TEAM 4 REALIZING A DREAM.

TJ QUEENS + KINGS: A2BEGJ2MOS2

TU QUEENS + KINGS: ABC2J2ITW

JOIN THE QC LEGACY △ GOT IDEAS? SIGN UP 4 PETITIONS ◊ GEAR ◊ BOOKS CALIFORNIA IS ME © CONTACT INFO
WWW.CALIFORNIAISME.COM ◊ WWW.CALIISME.COM
WWW.CALIFORNIAGREATSEAL.COM
◊ HTTPS://FACEBOOK.COM/CALIFORNIAISME
◊ HTTPS://TWITTER.COM/CALIFORNIAISME
TAMRA L. DICUS, FOUNDER AND OWNER
QUEENC@CALIISME.COM SUBJECT: QC2
P.O. BOX 25433, ALEXANDRIA, VA 22313

YOU'RE WELCOME.   AND STILL WE RISE ...

#TUSKEGEEALUMNI

QC² ISBN: 978-0-9742010-2-3
OTHER PUBLICATIONS BY CALIFORNIA IS ME®

WHO IS THE BLACK QUEEN CALAFIA OF GOLDEN CALIFORNIA?: THE REAL WONDER WOMAN
BY MS. TAMRA L. DICUS © 2018 ISBN-10 : 0974201014
ISBN-13 : 978-0974201016

THE QUEEN CALAFIA COVER-UP
BY MS. TAMRA L. DICUS COMING SOON.
ISBN: 978-0-9742010-3-0

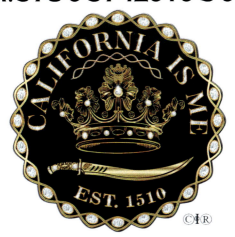

Made in the USA
Middletown, DE
12 November 2024